W9-CBC-828

Put Beginning Readers on the Right Track with
ALL ABOARD READING™

The All Aboard Reading series is especially for beginning readers. Written by noted authors and illustrated in full color, these are books that children really and truly *want* to read—books to excite their imagination, tickle their funny bone, expand their interests, and support their feelings. With four different reading levels, All Aboard Reading lets you choose which books are most appropriate for your children and their growing abilities.

Picture Readers—for Ages 3 to 6
Picture Readers have super-simple texts with many nouns appearing as rebus pictures. At the end of each book are 24 flash cards—on one side is the rebus picture; on the other side is the written-out word.

Level 1—for Preschool through First Grade Children
Level 1 books have very few lines per page, very large type, easy words, lots of repetition, and pictures with visual "cues" to help children figure out the words on the page.

Level 2—for First Grade to Third Grade Children
Level 2 books are printed in slightly smaller type than Level 1 books. The stories are more complex, but there is still lots of repetition in the text and many pictures. The sentences are quite simple and are broken up into short lines to make reading easier.

Level 3—for Second Grade through Third Grade Children
Level 3 books have considerably longer texts, use harder words and more complicated sentences.

All Aboard for happy reading!

With special thanks to
our editor, Jane O'Connor,
and art director, Ronnie Herman.

Library of Congress Cataloging-in-Publication Data

Dubowski, Cathy East.
    Pirate School / by Cathy East Dubowski ; illustrated by Mark Dubowski.
        p.   cm. — (All aboard reading)
    Summary: At Pirate School, Pete learns to act like a pirate and fight it out, but when he
and a classmate find the treasure at the same time, pirate rules don't seem to work.
    [1. Pirates—Fiction.   2. Schools—Fiction.   3. Treasure hunts—Fiction.]   I. Dubowski,
Mark, ill.   II. Title.   III. Series.
PZ7.D8544Pi   1996
    [E]—dc20   95-23241
                                                                                                         CIP
ISBN 0-448-41133-4 (GB)   A B C D E F G H I J   AC

ISBN 0-448-41132-6 (pbk.)   A B C D E F G H I J

ALL
ABOARD
READING™
Level 2
Grades 1-3

Pirate School

By Cathy East Dubowski
and Mark Dubowski

Grosset & Dunlap • New York

Pete's family

was a lot like other families.

Every morning

his mom and dad got breakfast.

His baby sister watched

Jolly Roger's Neighborhood.

And Pete rowed the bus

to school.

Pete went to school

on a ship.

The ship was called

P.S. 1.

The P.S. stood for

PIRATE SCHOOL!

Pete learned to add

by adding up gold coins.

He learned to subtract
by making classmates
walk the plank!

The kids at P.S. 1

were as hard as nails.

And so were the rules.

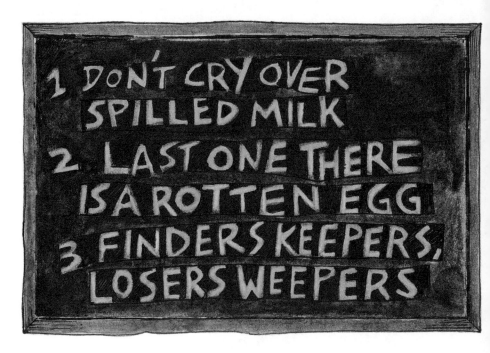

1. DON'T CRY OVER SPILLED MILK

2. LAST ONE THERE IS A ROTTEN EGG

3. FINDERS KEEPERS, LOSERS WEEPERS

Pete liked everything

about Pirate School.

Well, almost everything…

He hated Gregory Grimes the 13th!

(The kids called him Grimy.)

And Grimy hated Pete right back!

"You're too little
to lift the anchor!"
said Grimy.
"You're too big
to get through the hatch!"
said Pete.

"You little shrimp!" shouted Grimy.

"You big whale!" shouted Pete.

"STOP THAT!" yelled their teacher,
Captain Bones.

Captain Bones did not like
kids to call each other names.
"Act like big pirates," he said.
"And <u>fight</u> it out!"

So they did.

Who won?

"I did!" said Grimy.

"No, I did!" said Pete.

At Pirate School

the biggest day of the year

was Treasure Hunt Day.

Captain Bones held up a map.

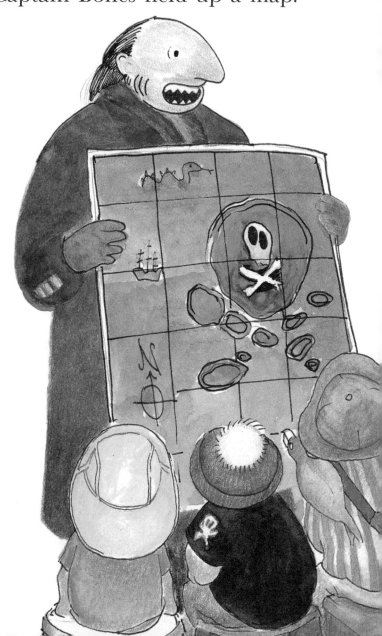

"The treasure is hidden here,"

he said.

"X marks the spot.

Find it,

and you get to keep it."

"Finders keepers!" hissed Grimy.

"Losers weepers!" snapped Pete.

All the kids rowed

to the shores of Skull Island.

Pete and Grimy fought all the way.

"I'm going to find

the treasure first!" said Grimy.

"No, I'm going to find it first!"

said Pete.

On Skull Island the class split up.

They all ran off to find

the X that marked the spot.

Pete looked high.

Pete looked low.

"I've got to find that X

before Grimy," he thought.

Pete went deeper and deeper
into the woods.

"That X could be anywhere,"
he said.

So he looked everywhere!

No luck!

At last he sat

down to think.

Suddenly he felt as if

someone was watching him.

Slowly he turned around....

23

"The X!" he cried.

"I found the X!

It looks just like the one on the map!"

"Forget it!" somebody yelled.

"I found it first!"

It was Grimy!

They had found the X

at the same time!

It was on the side

of an old ship.

"Scram!" said Grimy.

"The treasure is mine!"

"You want to fight about it?"

said Pete.

So they did.

Captain Bones would have been proud.

CRASH!

Pete and Grimy

fell through the rotted deck!

Down, down they went

into the dark!

Pete and Grimy hit bottom.

It was dark and wet and smelly.

Slowly their eyes
got used to the dark.

"L-look!" said Pete.

It was the treasure!

"We found it!" they cheered.

But then they stopped cheering.

They looked around.

There were no steps.

No ladder.

No rope. No door.

They were trapped!

"We'll never get out!"

cried Grimy.

"We'll starve to death.

By the time they find us,

we'll be a pile of bones!"

Pete and Grimy sat down

on the treasure

and waited to die.

"Hey, Pete," said Grimy.

"Are you scared?"

Pete nodded.

"Well, I'm more scared

than you!" said Grimy.

"No, I'm more scared

than you!" said Pete.

But before they could fight it out,

Pete got an idea.

First he got Grimy to help him

turn the treasure chest on its side.

Then he made Grimy

stand on top of the chest.

Then Pete stood on top of Grimy.

"Give me a boost!" Pete cried.

Grimy did.

Pete hit the deck with a thud.

"Ouch!" he said. "I made it!"

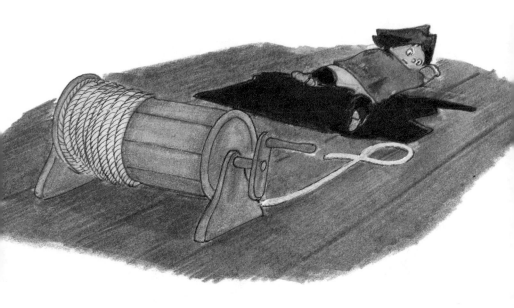

He grabbed a rope.

"Tie this to the treasure!"

he called down to Grimy.

Pete turned the crank

and pulled the treasure up.

Pete couldn't wait

to see what was inside.

He opened the chest.

"Wow!" he cried.

He had never seen so much treasure!

"And it's mine!" he shouted.

"All mine!"

"Hey, Pete!" called Grimy.

"What about ME?"

Pete looked down

into the big, dark hole.

Suddenly he had a terrible idea.

"I could just leave him there,"

he thought.

"He'd be a pile of bones.

And I would have all the treasure!"

"Aw, shellfish!" said Pete.

"I just can't do it!

If it weren't for Grimy's help,

I'd still be stuck down there, too."

So he threw down the rope

and pulled Grimy out.

"Thanks, mate," said Grimy.

"I was scared you were

going to leave me."

"No, I couldn't do that," said Pete.

"But don't tell Captain Bones

that I saved you.

He'd be mad!"

Together they carried the treasure

back to their boat.

Back at the ship

all the kids cheered.

But Captain Bones frowned.

"We have never had a tie before,"

he said.

"I guess there is only
one thing to do.
Act like big pirates
and fight it out!"

But Pete and Grimy had a better idea.

"We want to split it," said Pete.

"Fifty-fifty," said Grimy.

"Even Steven," said Pete.

So they did.

And that worked out great—

until there was just one coin left.

Pete and Grimy looked at it.

Everyone looked at Pete and Grimy.

What would they do now?

Were they going to fight it out?

No!

They flipped for it!